1-28-08

# Spider Storch's Desperate Deal

## Gina Willner-Pardo
### illustrated by Nick Sharratt

Albert Whitman & Company • Morton Grove, Illinois

Library of Congress Cataloging-in-Publication Data

Willner-Pardo, Gina.
Spider Storch's desperate deal / written by
Gina Willner-Pardo; illustrated by Nick Sharratt.
p. cm.
*Summary:* Third grader Spider Storch tries to keep his friends
from finding out that he has to be the ring bearer in a wedding
where the horrible Mary Grace Brennerman will be the flower girl.
ISBN 0-8075-7588-7 (hardcover)
ISBN 0-8075-7589-5 (paperback)
[1. Weddings—Fiction.] I. Sharratt, Nick, ill. II. Title.
PZ7.W683675Spd 1999
[Fic]—dc21
99-20140
CIP

Designed by Scott Piehl.

To Jerry. — G. W.-P.

For the Val d' Isère team. — N. S.

Don't forget to read . . .

Spider Storch's
# Teacher Torture

Spider Storch's
# Carpool Catastrophe

Spider Storch's
# Music Mess

Spider Storch's
# Fumbled Field Trip

by Gina Willner-Pardo
illustrated by Nick Sharratt

# Contents

# 1

# The World's Scariest Flower Girl

"Guess what?" Mary Grace Brennerman said.

Zachary and Andrew and I were seeing how many dominoes we could stack on top of each other. Mary Grace is always talking when I'm trying to concentrate.

"I'm going to be a flower girl in my mom's wedding," Mary Grace said.

"Who cares?" Zachary said.

"Flower girls are the most important part of a wedding," Mary Grace said. "More important than the bride, even."

"Careful, Spider," Andrew said. "We're up to domino number forty. Don't blow it."

Spider is my nickname. I like spiders more than basketball or video games or ice cream with sprinkles. Every Halloween I wear a spider costume, except one year when I went as a centipede. I even have spider underwear.

"I won't blow it," I said, "if she'll just shut up."

"Flower girls get to walk down the aisle first," Mary Grace said. "They get to throw rose petals and wear poufy dresses."

She held out her arms like a ballerina.

Forty dominoes make a lot of noise when they fall down all at once.

"You ruined our domino tower!" I yelled.

I was mad but not surprised. Mary Grace has been ruining stuff since kindergarten.

"Thanks a lot, Mary Grace," I said. "You big Sturgeon Breath."

"Joey Storch," she said, "you quit calling me that!"

I'd been calling Mary Grace Sturgeon Breath since we saw a

sturgeon when we went on a field trip.
I couldn't help it. That sturgeon
looked awful.

•

"Hey, Spider, can you imagine
anything scarier than Mary Grace
Brennerman in a poufy dress?"
Zachary asked as Ms. Schmidt led us
to the library.

"How about the bride of
Frankenstein's head in your
lunchbox?" Andrew said.

"Can you imagine anyone
ever *marrying* her?" Zachary asked.

Ms. Schmidt shushed us at the
library door.

"I'd rather marry the bride of
Frankenstein," I said.

# 2

# Do Ring Bears Roar?

"I have some exciting news," Mom said that night. We were eating dessert.

"Ooh, Mom, what?" my sister Louise said.

"Diane and Frank are getting married," Mom said.

"No kidding," Dad said. "Good for them!"

Frank was a mailman. I was always asking him for a ride in his truck, but he said it was against the rules. Otherwise he was pretty nice. Mrs. Brennerman was great. It was really hard to believe she was even related to Mary Grace.

I scraped cake and strawberry off

my whipped cream and shoveled as much as I could into my mouth.

"Mary Grace already told me," I said. "That's not exciting news."

Exciting news was when I found a water spider at camp, or the time Grandma Essie cracked up her car.

"Joey, how about swallowing

whatever's in your mouth before you speak?" Dad said.

"Did Mary Grace mention that I'm going to be a bridesmaid?" Mom asked.

"Ooh, Mom, how cool!" Louise said.

"Aren't you too old for that?" I asked.

"Certainly not," Dad said. "Your mother will be a spectacular bridesmaid." He gave her a big, dopey smile. Then he started asking a lot of questions about who was going to pay for the dress.

"And that's not all," Mom said.

"Guess who's going to be the ring bearer?"

"What's a ring bear?" I asked.

"Ring *bearer*. The boy who carries the wedding ring down the aisle," Louise said, like only dumb people didn't know.

"Why can't the married guy just carry it himself?" I asked.

"I have a feeling you'd better get the hang of this ring bearer thing, Joey," Dad said.

"Why?"

"Because *you're* going to be the ring bearer," Louise said.

"Me? I'm not being a ring bearer."

"Sure you are," Mom said.

"Me? In a wedding?" This was terrible. This was worse than terrible.

"Why can't Louise do it?"

"It has to be a boy," Mom said.

"Well, why can't Dad do it?"

"A *boy*, not a man," Louise said. "He's too old."

"All I know is, *I'm* not doing it," I said. "Weddings are for girls."

Mom stood up and put her hands on her hips. "Joseph Wolfgang Storch!" she said. "That is the most ridiculous thing I've ever heard. Who do you think girls marry?"

"Cheer up, Joey," Dad called from the sink. "Weddings are fun. You get to eat cake. You get to throw rice at people."

"You get to dance," Louise said dreamily.

She had a crush on Jason Nimowitz who lived next door. Jason was fourteen. He had a skateboard and pimples.

"Kids always have a grand time at weddings," Mom said. "You and Mary Grace will have a blast."

"Hey! Wait a minute!" I'd forgotten about Mary Grace. "You mean I have to do this with *her?*"

"Well, of course, sweetie," Mom said. "You'll look so cute together, all dressed up."

"No way."

Louise was laughing so hard she was spitting strawberries. "Maybe it'll be in the Sunday paper," Mom said.

*"Mom!"* I yelled. *"I am not being a ring bear!"*

Mom looked at me. I had never seen that look before. Not even when she called me Joseph Wolfgang Storch. "Oh, yes you are," she said.

I knew right then that I was doomed. I was going to be a ring bear. Mary Grace was going to be a flower girl and wear a poufy dress.

And everyone would know.

# 3

# Mary Grace Cuts a Deal

As I lay in bed, I decided there was only one thing to do. I had to make sure that no one found out about Mary Grace and me being in the wedding. If no one found out, no one could tease me.

I rolled over and tried to sleep. I felt a little better, except for wondering if the ring bearer was supposed to kiss the flower girl. That was so sickening, I made myself think about spiders instead.

•

At school I only talk to Mary Grace in emergencies. I decided to keep quiet until after school, when we waited at the dry cleaner's for Mrs. Brennerman to pick us up. Unfortunately, I am stuck carpooling with the Brennermans.

Mary Grace was already in front of the dry cleaner's when I got there.

"I have to talk to you," I said, "about being a ring bearer."

Mary Grace sighed.

"I tried to talk Mom out of it," she said. "I told her you'd probably put spiders in the crab puffs or knock over a candle and set the whole place on fire."

"Hey!" I said. "I almost never knock stuff over."

"What about the ant farm in first grade? What about the Statue of Liberty Travis Hoffberg made out of  toothpicks? What about Ms. Schmidt's nail polish remover?"

"I said *almost* never."

Mary Grace looked at herself in the dry cleaner's window like she was looking in a mirror. She patted at her hair and then turned around. "What *do* you want?" she asked.

I took a deep breath. "For you
not to tell anyone about me being
in the wedding."

"What do you care?"

"I don't want kids to tease us about
being in a wedding together."

"Who cares what dumb old kids
say? Sticks and stones can break my
bones, but words can never hurt me."

Boy, did she get on my nerves.
"Nobody believes that,"
I said.

"Some people do.
Mature, responsible
people. People like me," Mary Grace
said. "Ms. Schmidt is always saying
what an excellent attitude I have and
how grownup I act compared to
everyone else."

"Ms. Schmidt never says that."

Mary Grace smiled in an evil way.
"How much do you care what kids
say?" she asked.

"A lot."

"How much?"

Uh-oh, I thought. "Pretty much."

"How much is pretty much?" Mary
Grace asked. "You want me to keep
quiet about you being in this wedding.
Maybe there's something *I* want from
*you*." She paused. "Maybe a few
things."

"Like what?" I asked. My voice wobbled.

Mrs. Brennerman's van pulled up to the curb. Mary Grace slid the back door open.

"I'll let you know," she said.

# 4

# A Deal's a Deal

It took her two days to get back to me.

"I don't want you making fun of me ever again," she finally said in front of the dry cleaner's. "Don't call me names."

"What about sticks and stones?" I asked. "I thought you said mature kids didn't care about that stuff."

"No more Mary Grace the big Smelly Face. No more Sturgeon

Breath. No more Sasquatch."

"But—"

"Don't tell me that Michael Jordan
is your uncle. Don't say
'Open your mouth and
close your eyes, and I'll
give you a big surprise.'
Don't start a rumor that
my real parents sold me to the
Brennermans and then went into
the witness protection program!"
Mary Grace was turning red.

"All right, all right!"

"Just say, 'Hi, Mary Grace' when
you see me in the halls. Or 'That's a
really nice outfit, Mary Grace.' Or—"

"Are you nuts? Why? I don't say hi
to Zachary and Andrew, and they're
my best friends. I just walk up and
start talking."

Mary Grace looked all snooty. "Okay, then, why can't you just walk up and start talking to me?"

*"Because I hate you!"* I yelled. "And you hate me."

Mary Grace seemed to be thinking this over. "Well, then, just don't say anything," she finally said.

"Fine," I said. But after a minute, I asked, "Forever?"

"Yes, forever!" Mary Grace said.

"Or I'll tell. I'll tell everything. How we have to walk down the aisle together, and stand next to each other for pictures, and—"

I swallowed. "We have to do that stuff?"

Mary Grace nodded. "And you

have to *smile* the whole time, Joey, like you're having a good time."

"Okay," I said, "so we're even? I'll stop calling you names and saying creepy stuff, and you won't tell about me being a ring bearer?"

"Who said anything about even?" Mary Grace said. She watched as the van pulled up. "I'm still making a list."

"A list? What list?"

"A list of demands," Mary Grace said as she disappeared into the van.

She sounded like a spy. I felt the hair stand up on the back of my neck.

# 5

## What Mary Grace Wants

The next day was tough. Mary Grace blew her nose about twenty times during Free Reading. Zachary and Andrew kept looking at me and giggling. I bit my lip to keep myself from laughing.

At recess, Zachary wanted to follow Mary Grace around yelling, "Thar she blows!" but I said I wanted to work on lay-ups instead.

"What's the matter with you?" Zachary said. "Don't you know what 'Thar she blows' means? It's what whale hunters used to yell when they saw a whale spouting water."

"I'm just sick of Mary Grace," I said. "Do you want to play basketball or don't you?"

They did. I could feel them staring at the back of my neck as we headed across the playground to the hoops. We passed the third-grade girls playing four-square. I felt itchy with wanting to yell, "Thar she blows!" at Mary Grace.

•

At the end of lunch recess, we lined up to walk down the hall. Mary Grace got behind me.

"P.E.'s next," she whispered.

"So?"

"So," Mary Grace whispered, "you're always team captain in kickball."

"Yeah. So?"

"So," Mary Grace said, "pick me first."

"What?"

"Pick me to be on your team," she said. "It's what I want."

"I can't pick you," I said.

*"It's what I want,"* she said again. She had a really good way of yelling and whispering at the same time.

"All *right*. Are we even now?"

More silence. "I haven't decided," Mary Grace said, finally.

Which was her way of saying no.

•

We lost 14-3. Mary Grace didn't kick one ball. We made her stand way out in center field, but she yakked the whole time anyway. Even when Mary Grace stinks at something, she still wants to tell everyone else how to do it.

"Why did you go and do a stupid thing like picking Mary Grace?"

Andrew asked. "Mary Grace can't
kick a ball."

"Mary Grace can barely walk,"
Zachary said. "She can barely hold
a pencil without sweating and
breathing hard."

"I don't know," I said miserably.
"I felt sorry for her, I guess."

"Why do you feel sorry for her?"
Zachary shrieked. "Ms. Schmidt
always lets a girl be one of the team
captains. The girl team captain would
pick Mary Grace."

"I think Mary Grace is getting a
little better at running," I said.

"I noticed at recess. Those bony knees probably come in handy."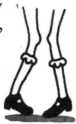

Andrew shook his head. "You're crazy, Spider," he said. "You're wacko."

I nodded and looked at my shoes. He was right. I was crazy.

Drat that Mary Grace, I thought. Making me lie to my best friends. In my head, I called her big Smelly Face about four hundred times.

# Bunny Hop

"Joey," Mary Grace said, "we need some boys."

"For what?" I asked. "Dessert?"

"No," Mary Grace said. "For our play."

Mary Grace likes to put on plays with the other third-grade girls. Mainly, she just likes bossing everybody around.

"It's called 'The Ducks and the Bunnies,'" Mary Grace said as we headed down the hall toward the playground. "I am Mother Bunny. We need boys for the boy parts."

"They'll say no," I said. "Boys would rather drop dead than be in a play about bunnies."

"It's what I want."

"But—"

"Just tell Zachary and Andrew to meet us over by the baseball diamond at first recess," Mary Grace said. "Zachary can be Papa Bunny. You would make a great Farmer McCoy."

*"Zachary? Papa Bunny?* What planet are you on?"

*"It's what I want,"* she said.

•

"Quit yanking on my arm, Mary Grace!" Zachary moaned.

"Oh, Papa, you're so cranky!" Mary Grace squealed in her bunny voice. In her regular, crummy-girl voice she said, "Come on, Zachary. You have to *hop*!"

"I *am* hopping!"

"That's not hopping," Mary Grace said. "That's *skipping*!"

"Hey, Mary Grace," Andrew called from somewhere out past third base. "How long do I have to stand out here?"

"You're not *supposed* to be *standing*." Mary Grace sounded impatient. "You're Grandpa Quackers and you're guarding the eggs while Mrs. Fuzzy Fluff takes a walk."

"Yeah!" said Regina. "I've been sitting on those eggs all winter. I need a break."

"This is stupid," Zachary said. "I'm not playing anymore."

Mary Grace shot me a look. I put down the stick that was supposed to be my pitchfork and walked over to the dugout.

"Come on, Zachary," I said. "Just a few more minutes."

"What's with you, Spider?" Zachary said.

"Yeah." Andrew was walking toward me from third base. "What's gotten into you, anyway?"

"Nothing's gotten into me." They were both standing close enough to hear me whisper. "I already told you. I just think we should practice being in a play. For a little while. In fourth grade there's a *real* play, with a stage and costumes. We might get to be pirates."

"How do you know?" Andrew asked.

"Louise says the fourth-grade play is always about pirates," I whispered.

"I don't see how hopping is good practice for being a pirate," Zachary grumbled.

"You better be right,"

Andrew said. If I didn't know he was my friend, I'd have thought he looked mad.

"You better know what you're doing, Spider."

# 7

# Tuxedo Junction

I was so glad it was the weekend. No Mary Grace. No list of demands. No ducks and bunnies.

"Guess what, Joey?" Mom said at lunch. "Today we're shopping for your tuxedo!"

"What's a tuxedo?"

"A fancy suit," Mom said. "Frank wants to meet us down at the tuxedo rental store to make sure your suit matches his."

"*Rental?*"

"That's right," Mom said.

"You mean I have to wear someone else's clothes?" I said. "Clothes that someone else got all sweaty?"

"The store cleans all the clothes, Joey—"

"This stinks," I said. "This is gross."

Mom sat down next to me on the couch.

"This is how weddings are, Joey," she said. "Really. Most of the time, men and boys rent tuxedos."

I leaned my head against her shoulder. "It just makes me sick, thinking about my body in someone

43

else's pants," I said. "Do I get to wear my own underwear?"

"Of course," Mom said.

"Well," I said, "that's something."

•

Frank the mailman met us at  Tuxedo Junction.

"How's my ring bearer?" he asked. He sounded happy.

"You look different without your uniform," I said.

"Amazing, isn't it?" Frank said. "Not all my clothes are gray."

"Okay, Joey," Mom said. "Mr. Petropoulos needs to measure you now."

I looked back at the two of them as Mr. Petropoulos led me to a dressing room. Frank stood straight and saluted. "Courage, mate!" he called. Mom waggled her fingers at me.

Mr. Petropoulos had hairy knuckles and smelled like bathroom tile cleaner. He measured me practically everywhere and wrote all the numbers down. Finally he put his tape measure away and left the dressing room. He came back with a black tuxedo, black socks, and black shoes that looked like the ones Dad wears to work.

"I hope I don't get foot fungus from

these socks," I said. "My dad had that once. One of his toenails turned black and fell off."

Mr. Petropoulos made a "tsk tsk" sound with his tongue. "You put these on," he said. "Come out when you're dressed. Show me and your mama how you look."

Everything fit, except for a piece of shiny, red cloth. I didn't know what it was for, but I figured it would make a pretty good pirate eyepatch.

"Is this right?" I asked, stepping out of the dressing room.

"Oh, Joey," Mom said.

I could tell from the way her eyes crinkled that she was trying not to laugh.

"That's a cummerbund. It goes around your waist."

She took the red thing off my head. "Like this."

"No. Leave it," Frank said. "I like it Joey's way. I'm going to wear my cummerbund like that."

"This looks stupid," I said, seeing myself in the mirror. "This red thing looks like something a girl would wear."

"I think you look like a soldier in olden times," Frank said. He cocked his head. "See, you could keep your weapon hidden under your cummerbund."

"Please don't give him any ideas," Mom said.

●

After trying on suits, Frank asked Mom if he could take me out for ice cream.

"In the mail truck?" I asked.

"You know the rules, Joey," he said. "I took the bus."

We walked to the ice cream parlor. Frank had a root beer float. I ordered a double scoop of chocolate chip with sprinkles.

Something about the way Frank made noise when he used his straw made me think I could talk to him.

"There's this girl at school," I said. "She never thinks I'm funny. She's been mad at me for as long as I've known her." I was careful not to say it was Mary Grace. I didn't want Frank blabbing to Mrs. Brennerman. "She's trying to make me change."

"No one can make you do anything

you don't want to do," Frank said.

"She knows something about me,"
I said. "Something I don't want her to
tell."

"When I was a kid, my mom made
me take tap dancing lessons," Frank
said. "And Howard Springer found
out."

"Who's Howard Springer?"

"This really mean kid. He had a

mustache in fifth grade.
Anyway, he told me he was
going to tell the whole
school about me taking tap
dancing lessons unless I
bought him a skateboard."

"What a jerk."

"You're not kidding. I was going to
do it, too. I really didn't want anyone
knowing about the tap dancing."

My mom loved old movies with tap dancing. I could see her getting ideas. I shivered. "So, what happened?"

"I couldn't save up enough money for the skateboard, so Howard told everyone. Just like he said he would," Frank said. "For months, every time I walked into a room, everyone would stamp their feet on the floor."

"You should have quit tap dancing," I said. "That would have solved everything."

Frank slurped up the last of his float.

"Except I really liked tap dancing," he said.

"You did?"

"A lot," he said. "You got to make noise without everyone telling you to be quiet."

I never thought of that.

"Plus I didn't like someone telling me what to do," Frank said.

I shoved what was left of my ice cream cone into my mouth so Frank wouldn't see how much he was making me think.

# Here Comes the
# Ring Bear!

"Joey!" Mary Grace called. "Wait up!"

"Why is she always talking to you all of a sudden?" Andrew asked.

"I am not, repeat, *not*, going to spend my lunch recess hopping around in the bushes and saying things like, 'Who stole my carrots?'"

Zachary said. "Just so you know."

He and Andrew kept walking while I stopped for Mary Grace.

"Now what?" I asked. "Listen, Mary Grace, you have to stop talking to me all the time. Zachary and Andrew are getting suspicious."

"Does Zachary ever say anything else?" Mary Grace asked. "About me, I mean."

"What are you talking about?"

"I would like it," Mary Grace said, "if you said something nice about me to him, and then told me what he said back. Tell him I have pretty hair. Or nice eyes. Or a great smile."

"You're *crazy*, Mary Grace."

"Maybe he thinks I have pretty hair and he's just never said anything to you about it."

"Zachary? Zachary wipes boogers under the seats of chairs. Zachary couldn't care less about pretty hair."

"Just find out," Mary Grace said as she skipped away.

•

The morning of the wedding, as Mary Grace and I waited to walk down the aisle of the church, I whispered, "I'm not asking Zachary about your dumb old hair."

Someone started playing the piano.

"Joey Storch, you better do what I say," Mary Grace hissed. She was busy trying to look pretty and making sure her little sister Angel didn't suck her thumb, but she still managed to sound bossy.

"I don't care what you do to me. Tell everyone in the world about the wedding," I said. "You dumb old Sasquatch."

I felt like someone had let me out of a cage or taken handcuffs off my wrists. I felt wonderful.

Mom gave Mary Grace and Angel baskets full of flower petals. She handed me

a red velvet box with Mrs.
Brennerman's ring inside.

"Okay, kids," she whispered, her
face all smiley. She looked pretty,
for a mom. "You're on."

Mary Grace and Angel and I
walked down the aisle together.
It wasn't nearly as hard as I thought
it would be. It was fun, everybody
staring at us. Except for Angel eating
a big clump of her petals and Mary

Grace giving me dirty looks,
everything went like clockwork.

Nobody knew about the water gun
I hid under my cummerbund. Frank
was right. It fit perfectly.

Mrs. Brennerman and Frank held
hands and smiled while Reverend
Carleton said a lot of disgusting stuff
about loving each other. Then
Frank said some stuff just to Mrs.
Brennerman. I didn't understand
what he said, but her eyes got shiny.

After everyone did a lot more
talking, Reverend Carleton asked me
for the ring. I was keeping it in my
pocket so I wouldn't lose it, along with
a gumball, two rubberbands, a piece
of duct tape, seven plastic
spiders, and an old
Christmas ornament

that I'd found under my bed that morning. I had to dig around for the ring box; the gumball, the ornament, and some of the spiders fell out of my pocket while I was doing it. Everybody laughed, except for Mary Grace, who looked disgusted, and my mom, who looked like she wanted to move to another state.

The guests clapped and cheered when Mrs. Brennerman and Frank kissed. Then we all walked out of the church and stood around. A man took pictures. He made Mary Grace and Angel and me pose for one. Angel kept trying to hold my hand.

Later, at the Community Center where the party was, I said to Mom, "How come you didn't tell me there

was a band? I could have brought my flute."

"Listen, Joey," Mom said, "ask Angel to dance."

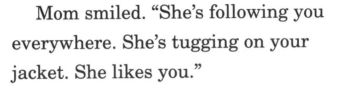

"What?"

Mom smiled. "She's following you everywhere. She's tugging on your jacket. She likes you."

"She's *two*," I said. "She's not even a person."

"Of course she is," Mom said. "Do it for me."

I thought about how Mom had looked when I was trying to find the ring.

"Okay," I mumbled. "But this better be the last thing I have to do today."

"It won't be as hard as you think," Mom said.

"Thank you, Joey."

I didn't really dance. I just stood on the dance floor while Angel ran around me.

Everyone was smiling, even the musicians.

It was awful.

•

I didn't take my water gun out until later, when Mary Grace went up to the buffet for seconds of spareribs. Maybe it was thirds. Mary Grace eats like a horse.

I only wanted to get her a little wet. I aimed right at her, but I missed and hit the tray of spareribs instead.

"That's it, Joey!" she said, after my mom had wiped the splats of barbecue sauce off her poufy dress and confiscated my gun. "On Monday I'm

telling. I'm saying you asked me
to dance. How when we posed for
pictures you tried to hold my hand."

"Tell them I proposed to you,"
I said. "You big Smelly Face."

"I thought you didn't want anyone
to know about you being a ring
bearer," Mary Grace said.

"I guess I don't care as much as
I thought," I said, shoving more cake
into my mouth. "I'm getting older.
More mature."

"Now I've got frosting on my shoes!" Mary Grace leaned down and tried to wipe her shoes with her napkin.

While she wasn't looking, I pulled a couple of plastic spiders out of my pocket and arranged them in the frosting on her slice of cake. They looked real. I couldn't wait for her to sit up and scream.

"I don't care what you tell people." It didn't matter. She couldn't make me do anything I didn't want to do.

I felt a hand on my back.

"Joey," Mrs. Brennerman said, "Frank and I want to talk to you and Mary Grace."

Did she see the spiders? Was she mad at me for spoiling everything?

"Nice wedding, Mrs. Brennerman,"
I said. "You look really pretty."

She smiled. "Mrs. *Withers*
now," she said. "Come on,
you guys. Frank and I have
a surprise."

Mary Grace stood
up without even
noticing the spiders.

•

Someone had tied ribbons and
crepe paper and tin cans onto the
bumpers of Frank's mail truck. And
there was a sign that had been stuck
onto the rear license plate that said,
"Neither rain nor sleet nor dead of
night..." Pink-and-white balloons
were tied to the radio antenna.

"Hop in, kids!" Frank said.
"Once around the block!"

"Really?" I asked. "Really?"

"Just a quick ride," Frank said. "Come on."

"I'm not getting in that thing with him," Mary Grace said. "Look what he did to my dress! And besides, that truck has open sides. My hair'll get all messy."

"Oh, come on, Mary Grace," I said. For some reason, I really wanted her to go.

Mary Grace crossed her arms and clamped her mouth shut.

"Come on," I said again.

I thought about what I could say that was true. I couldn't tell her that I wouldn't make fun of her or call her names or tell people I hated her. I knew that I would, no matter how hard I tried not to. "Your hair will still look pretty even if it's all blown around," I said.

Mary Grace sort of smiled. "You're still the most disgusting boy in third grade, Joey Storch," she said as she climbed into the mail truck.

"And you're still a dumb old Sturgeon Breath," I said.

The engine rumbled beneath us. It was weird. For a second, hating

Mary Grace felt an awful lot like liking her.

•

The kids all thought my being in a wedding with Mary Grace was hilarious. Everyone laughed and said what a cute couple we were. Regina hummed "Here Comes the Bride" every time she saw me.

"You and Mary Grace?" Zachary shrieked, holding his stomach. "In a wedding? Together?"

"It wasn't so bad," I said. "Except when I used Mrs. Brennerman's dress to wipe barbecue sauce off my hands."

"Why'd you do that?" Andrew asked.

"She was standing right next to me. Her skirt was almost in my lap. I thought it was my napkin," I said. "It was an honest mistake."

"I bet your mom didn't think so," Andrew said.

I had tried to explain to her that at least I was wiping my hands, but I don't think Mom even heard me.

"I've never seen her get so red," I said.

Zachary was laughing so hard
he could barely talk.

"I wish I'd been there," he kept
saying. "You and Mary Grace in a
wedding. That's something I'd have
liked to see."

It really got on my nerves. I
thought about telling him that
Mary Grace wanted him to like
her hair. There was a lot more I
could have said, too. How she wanted
him to run his fingers in it. How she

washed it and thought of him.

But I didn't. I just kept smiling and nodding.

It wasn't as hard as I thought.